The Red-Hot Pepper Fiasco

THE CACTUSVILLE KIDS

The
Red-Hot Pepper
Fiasco

PATRICIA HICKMAN
Illustrated by Taia Morley

Augsburg
MINNEAPOLIS

THE RED-HOT PEPPER FIASCO

Library of Congress Cataloging-in-Publication Data

Hickman, Patricia.
    The red hot pepper fiasco / Patricia Hickman ; illustrated by Taia
Morley.
    p. cm. -- (The Cactusville kids)
    Summary: Child actor Moon Holly moves from Los Angeles to Cactusville,
Arizona, where she makes new friends, forms a club, tries to earn money for a pony,
and learns about Jesus.
    ISBN 0-8066-2737-9 (alk. paper)
    [1. Moving, Household--Fiction. 2. Friendship--Fiction.
3. Clubs--Fiction. 4. Ponies--Fiction. 5. Christian life--Fiction.]
I. Morley, Taia, ill. II. Title. III. Series:
Hickman, Patricia. Cactusville kids.
PZ7.H53145Re   1995
[Fic]--dc20
                      95-30736
                          CIP
                          AC

The paper used in this publication meets the minimum requirements of American National Standard for Information Sciences—Permanence of Paper for Printed Library Materials, ANSI Z329.48-1984.   ∞

Manufactured in the U.S.A.   AF 9-2737

99	98	97	96	95	1	2	3	4	5	6	7	8	9	10

To my son, Joshua, whose life reflects the tender mercy and love of our Savior. Always be a worshiper, son.

Contents

My Name Is Moon Holly

My mother wanted me to be a star my whole life! From the day I was born it was obvious. Who else would name a baby girl Moon Holly Soileau (that's "Swallow") except a starry-eyed lady dreaming in the back row of the movie theater of the day her girl would grow up to be famous? That's my mom.

From the time that I could sit up and say, "Goo-goo-gah-gah," I was being ushered in one talent agency and out the other.

My favorite place was the Starlight Talent Agency, which got acting jobs mostly for kids, and my favorite agent was Hubie Hoffmeister. He was a short guy who dressed in these really wild kind of duds.

Hubie was always giving advice like "Leave 'em laughing" and "Give 'em something to remember you by, kid."

Hubie always wanted to be remembered too, so he had himself a splashy jacket made with flashing lights. He wore it everywhere he went.

For blocks you could see Hubie's back all lit up and flashing "Starlight . . . Talent . . . Starlight . . . Talent."

One thing for sure, people remembered Hubie!

Hubie and I go *way* back. Once he even landed a television commercial job for me. All I had to do was sit and drool wearing nothing but a towel! Of course, that was when I was only one and a half, and I don't remember a thing.

The Starlight was a really busy place, and all the people always talked to me as though I were a grown-up. I made a lot of friends at the agency except with the gray-haired receptionist, Miss Cookie Sublime. I think that was her stage name back in the old days when show business was called vaudeville.

Miss Cookie was kind of grumpy—probably because she didn't ever get married or have any kids, Hubie said.

But she got worse the day I took all her paper clips out of a coffee mug that read "I brake for construction workers" and linked them all up into a chain—eight feet long—and then let my goldfish, Charlie Chaplin, take a swim in her glass of iced tea. It took a while to calm her down and coax her off the fire escape. Miss Cookie won't drink iced tea or eat fish to this day!

I'd learned to tap-dance fairly well, but singing was what I always dreamed of doing. I didn't care if I was singing in the shower, on the stage at auditions, or just singing in the rain. I just loved singing and even took a few lessons. My voice teacher said singing wasn't exactly my "forte," whatever that means, and suggested that I "branch out and try to find myself." So I soon "found myself" taking other things like water ballet. As a matter of fact, I've taken all different kinds of lessons—I've even learned a little karate. Hi-yah!

People always said I was kind of tall for my age (which is ten), and my height always made me look older when I was in pageants and recitals and talent shows. Because of my height and my "bubbling" personality, Mom said acting was my "destiny." Ho-hum!

But enough about my mother's dreams. I've had some of my own too.

It seemed for the longest time my whole life was surrounded by grown-ups. I used to beg my mother to move away from the city of Los Angeles, where we lived in a high-rise building called the Peabody Towers. There were a few other kids in the building; but I never saw them, except occasionally on the elevator.

So my first dream was to have a best friend. My second dream was a secret that nobody knew about—I wanted my very own pony.

One night I woke up feeling really sick. I couldn't breathe and my face turned blue. It scared my mother to death! Mom rushed me to the hospital. There they clamped an oxygen mask on my face and injected some clear stuff into my arm. For a while, I thought they were going to have to give my mother the oxygen mask, but she finally calmed down. I was so out of it I didn't even yell when they poked me.

A doctor came in and examined me. "I'm afraid we're going to have to run some more tests, Ms. Soileau," she told Mom.

The next week was a royal pain!

Another doctor gave me an allergy test. He had his nurse make ink marks all over my back. Then she poked my back with all sorts of needles and rubbed some liquid stuff all over. My back stung and itched, and some of the ink squares gave me big, hot, pink bumps.

After looking at the ink marks, the doctor said to my mother, "It looks as though your daughter has some allergies, which are giving her asthma."

"Asthma!" I croaked. All the kids with asthma that I knew were pale and wore glasses and sat inside all the time reading geography books!

But this was me—Moon Holly Soileau—with asthma! Didn't they know I had a lot of plans? Asthma just didn't fit in with my life at all!

Then the greatest thing happened that could possibly happen with this asthma business.

My mother heard that Arizona had dry air that might be great for asthmatics like me. She talked to her boss, and the next thing you know she got a transfer to Cactusville, Arizona! So it was good-bye Hollywood and hello Cactusville! Good-bye pollution and hello clean air! Good-bye concrete and hello—what? Cactuses? What was I getting myself into?

The Cactusville Raiders

Moving to a new town can be a little scary. So I decided that I would make a big adventure out of the move. It made me feel sort of like the good guys in an Indiana Jones movie. Mom and I were taking off on a new escapade. Who knew what dangers lurked ahead?

After telling some of my grown-up friends "so long" at the Starlight and saying good-bye to Hubie, I began packing up all the things that I had won, like trophies and plaques. It almost seemed silly to tote them around, but they were a big part of the only life I had ever known. Throwing them away seemed too much like throwing myself away.

So into a big cardboard box they all went, along with my dance leotards, tap shoes, and shiny doo-dads for my hair.

Mom and I loaded up everything we owned. Then we drove away in one of those do-it-yourself jobbies with the bright orange paint and a big mural of Alaska on the side—even though we weren't moving to Alaska.

The drive to Cactusville was great! We left so early the sun was just beginning to come up, and we got to see the most awesome sunrise ever. Then I got busy looking up facts in a book about Arizona. I looked for places to go and things to see.

While flipping through the pages and imagining myself a research journalist, my eyes fell on the most beautiful sight I had ever seen! It was a picture of a pony called Pony of the Americas. How patriotic can you get?

The pony was mostly white with small bright patches on its backside. It was standing next to a boy in native Indian clothing. The pony's big, gorgeous, brown eyes seemed to be looking straight at me and saying, "Take me home. Take me home, Moon Holly!"

It was love at first sight. Suddenly I had an idea.

"Mom, did you know they have horses in Arizona?" I decided to ease into the conversation slowly so as not to spook her. My mom is easy to spook if you just jump right in with something unexpectedly.

"Uh-huh." Her mind was miles away as she craned her neck, blonde ponytail wagging, looking for the next pit stop.

"I've never seen a real horse—you know, like up close and in person." I leaned back real casually.

"Uh, well, I used to have an aunt with a pony." Mom kept craning, her green eyes jumping from one sign to the next.

"You did?" That was great! Maybe Mom was a potential horse lover!

"Yeah, I tried to pet it once, and it bit the end off my tennis shoe. Horses can be dangerous."

Oh, no! It was probably crazy. Leave it to my mother to find the only loony horse in the whole world! "Well, they don't usually do that—do they?"

"I don't know. But they're smelly and make a big mess," she said. "You have to take care of them every day."

"Oh, but I would, Mom. Really I would!" Oops! Me and my big mouth! The cat—rather, the horse—was out of the bag now!

"What?" her voice almost croaked. "Buy a horse? I could never afford it."

"But, Mom . . ." I begged.

"No, Moon Holly! Forget it!" Her voice had that sound to it. You know, the "don't mess with me" sound. So I left it—for the time being.

We took Interstate Ten all the way to Arizona, but then we had to turn off to find Cactusville. Just as the sun was beginning to set, I was getting sleepy. I had to lie down on the seat to take a little cat nap. Suddenly I heard my mom's voice.

"There it is! Look, Moon!"

I stretched out my legs and sat up.

"Whoa, look at that!" A bright yellow sign in the shape of a cactus read, "Welcome to Cactusville." We pulled into town, and I looked all around at the little shops with green awnings. "A real town with no high-rises!" I was excited. "Where's our apartment?"

My mom smiled in a real funny way and kept driving.

The places we passed sure looked different—nothing like Los Angeles. When we pulled up to the gas station, we didn't even have to wait in line. And sure enough, right next to the station, hovering over a man sitting on a bench fast asleep, was the biggest, greenest cactus ever! Yep! We had found Cactusville all right!

Then Mom drove down some streets where we passed apartment buildings, but not ours. Soon she pulled into a neighborhood with houses that looked really different. She said they made houses differently here from those in Los Angeles. They used some stuff called stucco, which I called "stooso" by mistake.

"No, Moon," Mom corrected me, "it sounds like 'stucko'."

Then the wildest thing happened. Mom flipped on the turn

signal—which I called the clicker—and pulled right into the driveway of one of the houses. It was tan colored and had a red roof—a real "stucko" if I'd ever seen one!

"Whose house is this?" I asked.

"Ours!" she said laughing.

"A house?" I couldn't believe it! A real house with a yard and a fence in the back. That meant there was a small chance I could worm my way into having my own dog.

I jumped out of the rental van and ran into the front yard. My yard! There weren't any cactuses, but we could plant some. But there *were* these light green trees called cottonwoods. I ran into our backyard. For as far as I could see, there were people sitting around in lawn chairs having barbecues, and kids were everywhere!

I sucked in a nostril-full of air. It smelled okay. I thought it might be like clamping on the oxygen mask, but it wasn't. It smelled like . . . a neighborhood . . . like grass and dirt and smoked chickens.

Boy! If Hubie Hoffmeister were here, he would catch the fastest plane back to Los Angeles. But something about this place caused me to grin from ear to ear.

Little did I know that beyond my backyard lurked disaster!

Elmer the Fuddster

Did I mention that I had a purple streak in my hair?
While Mom was unlocking the front door, four kids gathered in the yard beside our house. They just stood there in their swimsuits staring at me! Finally I figured out it might have something to do with that purple streak. In Los Angeles, a purple streak was nothing compared to some of the wild hairdos that people wore.

But the streak wasn't my idea, and I certainly hadn't colored it myself. Before we left Los Angeles I had done a magazine layout for a company that sold kids' clothes. The clothes were really bright, and they wanted me to look kind of . . . well, hip . . . RAD!

The stylist told me the streak would wear out quickly, and it seemed to blend in a bit with my shoulder-length, dark brown hair. But the color was definitely purple. Suddenly it felt rather strange standing out there in the middle of Cactusville with purple hair. I kind of wondered later if the people of Cactusville thought maybe aliens from outer space had landed.

"Hey, what's your name?" one girl with long, blonde braids asked.

Oh, boy! Now they'll really think I'm weird. I waited and then decided to get it over with. "My name is Moon—Moon Holly Soileau."

They all looked at each other and then looked back at me. "Did you say your name is Moon?" one of the boys said sounding surprised. He stared at the other kids and poked his buddy in the ribs with his long, bony elbow.

I nodded.

I'll never forget that moment as long as I live. That boy's freckled face started scrunching up like he'd just sucked on a lemon. He even had yellowish eyes. He laughed out loud in one of those long, hacking laughs that draws attention for miles. I stood there taking it for a while. Then I decided to "take the bull by the horns," as they say in Cactusville.

"So, buster, what's your name?" I crossed my arms, made my eyes look real beady, and stared back, hopeful that his parents had given him some really goofy name like Wilbur or Starbuck.

He folded his arms back at me and stuck out his bottom lip. "My name is Elmer." He looked so proud. I almost felt guilty at the task that was set before me—but not *too* guilty.

"You mean . . . as in Fudd? Elmer Fudd?" I smiled slyly.

The other three kids with him—another boy with pointy lips and short, cropped, brown hair and the two girls—fell all over the place laughing. Elmer stood there glaring at me. His freckles heated up to a hot red, and his big, pale ears twitched.

"What's it to you, Moon Beam?" he said glaring. By the look on his face I could tell he felt he had cut me to the quick.

"That's Moon Holly, Elmer. Moon Beam sounds more like another cartoon character . . . like you!"

All the kids howled again, which set the neighborhood dogs to barking.

The girl with the braids tried to catch her breath. She walked over and held out her hand to me. "You're all right, Moon Holly! My name is Jessica. This is my friend, Betsy. We call her Bets. And that's Todd Tweetweiller." She pointed to the boy with the pointy lips.

Bets stepped forward. She had dark skin and looked like an American Indian. Her shiny, black hair had grown past her waist. Around her neck hung a sterling silver necklace with a turquoise cross on it. "Hi, Moon. It's nice to meet you. Is this your first time in Cactusville?"

"Yeah." I was grateful for the friendliness. "Say, Bets, have you ever thought of being in TV commercials?" I asked. "You have great hair!"

She laughed. "Me? On TV?" She wound up her hair and held it on top of her head with one hand while posing the other hand on her hip. "I'm the famous girl from the big city of Cactusville!" She smiled and batted her long eyelashes.

We all laughed then. Suddenly things were going so well, I decided I wouldn't spill my guts about my acting career. Then they might really think I was weird.

"Say," I had a sudden thought. "Do you guys have a horse?"

Bets shook her head. "No, but we rent horses and ride the trails down by the stables."

"Yeah, it's great!" Jessica exclaimed. "Why? Do you ride?"

There were a lot of things I could brag about doing, but horseback riding wasn't one of them. "No. But I really want to learn. I think I want to buy my own pony."

"You could afford that?" asked Bets.

"Why? Are they expensive?" I know I sounded really dumb at this point.

"They're pretty expensive!" Jessica seemed to know what she was talking about.

"Well, then," I decided kind of spur-of-the-moment, "I'll just have to raise the money."

Now that could pose a problem. Even the magazine ad money I'd made had already gone into a trust for my college fund. Sometimes Mom would hold out extra money for me if I really wanted something, like my skateboard. But enough for a pony? She would absolutely croak if I even mentioned it.

"Hey, I have an idea," Bets suddenly spoke up. "Jess and I are horse-crazy maniacs, and we've been thinking of forming a club. Since you're a horse lover too, maybe we could all be in a club together."

"Great idea, Bets," Jessica joined in. "It'll be a secret for us three. What'll we call ourselves?"

"How about the Girls-Only Saddle Club?" Bets decided.

Yuk! I thought to myself, but didn't want to ruin a perfectly new friendship by saying it out loud. "Wait a second! Let's give ourselves something really splashy!" It must have been Hollywood coming out in me, but I cupped my hand in the air like the agents do on TV (only they don't really do it in real life—except for Hubie if he's in a goofy mood). "Let's call ourselves The Cactusville Adventure Club!" Their eyebrows shot up. They were impressed!

"Absolutely fantastic!" Jessica jumped in the air.

"Incredible!" Bets' dark eyes flashed like marbles.

"But you have to help me get a pony, guys," I smiled hopefully.

Jessica threw her hand in the air for a high-five, and Bets jumped up to slap it excitedly.

"You got it, girlfriend!" Jessica smiled back at me, and we all did high-fives and laughed.

Todd, who'd been pretty quiet until then, whistled while "the Fuddster" Elmer yelled at Jessica and Bets, "Hey, let's go to my house and swim. Moon Beam needs to help her mommy move in."

The girls looked at me. "You guys go ahead," I said.

"We'll catch you later, they said." So with beach towels in hand, off ran Jessica and Bets with Elmer Fudd and his side-kick Tweety. Somewhere inside of me I felt this was the beginning of something I had needed for a long time—friendship.

Now if I could just come up with a way to buy myself a pony. One thing that Hubie had always told me was that where there was a will there was a way. That was easy for Hubie to say. But what *was* the way? The Cactusville Adventure Club definitely had its first big mission.

The Riding Lesson

J ust put your left foot in the stirrup and grab the horn."
Jessica made getting on a horse sound so easy.

It had taken three days to help Mom unpack the orange
Alaska truck, but then I was ready for my first horseback
lesson.

I had gotten up early on Wednesday morning to meet
Jessica and Bets at the Agape Stables. The Agape was a western riding club where you could pay five dollars and ride the
trails all day. The thirty-five dollar beginner lessons were
sounding better to me at this point.

"Okay, Jess, just give me a minute to figure this out. He
really looks big, doesn't he?" I was stalling.

"It's not a he, it's a she. Isn't she beautiful?" Jessica
beamed.

"She's a beauty all right." I faked a smile. My knees locked,
and I felt my heart beginning to flutter. "What kind of horse is
she?" Maybe this would take a while to explain.

"She's a quarter horse. Her name is Miss Molly, and she's
gentle as a lamb. Perfect for a greenhorn like you, Moon."

"Greenhorn!" Those were fighting words in my neck of the
Los Angeles woods. With one push I threw my leg up and over

the leather saddle and wrapped my stone-washed jeans around Miss Molly's girth—that's her middle—as tightly as I could. Miss Molly whinnied and made a small dust cloud with one front hoof.

Bets laughed. "Not so tight with your legs. Just let them relax a bit, and place your feet in the stirrups."

"Oh." I tried to smile. "What do I do with these?" I asked, holding up the reins, one in each hand.

"You use them to steer the horse." Jessica pointed to her own reins and mounted her horse, a pale palomino named Thunderhead.

Then Jessica took the reins, held them in her left hand, and pulled gently to the right. Making a clicking noise with her tongue, she nudged Thunderhead's flanks with the heel of her boots. Thunderhead made a snorting sound and then obediently turned to the right. He circled around me and Miss Molly and stopped in front of us again.

"You just hold them with one hand?" I asked, holding up the reins with my left hand.

"You got it, girlfriend!" Bets smiled and mounted her horse, a black beauty named Anasazi, which was the name of a Native American tribe in Arizona.

"Isn't it funny how you both got horses that look like you?" I scratched my head.

"What about you?" Jessica answered flatly. "Moon Holly sounds like Miss Molly!"

"You girls ready to go?" I heard a man's voice say from behind us.

"Hi, Buck!" Jessica and Bets smiled at the man in the cowboy hat.

Jessica pointed to me. "This is our friend, Moon Holly. Hey, Moon! Meet Buck. He runs the stables."

I smiled at Buck. His big, white teeth grinned from a tanned, leathery face. He wore a light-colored felt hat and a blue chambray shirt with a cross and the name of the stables embroidered on the pocket. He wouldn't have fit in at all at the Starlight Talent Agency or the Peabody Towers in L.A. But he looked natural standing there with the stables and the tumbleweeds behind him. "It's nice to meet you, Buck," I said in a friendly way.

"Pray for her, Buck," Bets sounded dramatic. "She'll need it."

"Prayer?" I couldn't believe my ears. "You have no faith in me?" I held my hand up to my forehead and looked forlorn, as my acting teacher had once told me to do.

"It's not that." Bets winked at Jess and Buck. "I just have great faith in God!"

Oh. I thought. I didn't know much about God, but I was glad to take all the help I could get.

Buck walked over and patted my horse on the neck. "She's a good one to learn on. If anyone can teach you to ride western, it's these two cowgirls here," he said, pointing to Jessica and Bets. "But before you girls take off, let's pray."

Everyone bowed their heads, so I did too. Buck prayed, "Dear Lord," and his face suddenly looked softer. "Keep these cowgirls safe today. Help them to find the right path and stay on it. In Jesus' name, Amen." He smiled at me again.

This was for sure the happiest bunch of people I had ever seen. "Say, Buck!" I yelled.

"Yes, ma'am," he smiled politely.

"Is it hard to find the right trail?" I asked wondering about his prayer.

Then he did something kind of strange. He winked at the girls, and they all giggled like they knew a big secret.

"Let's go, girlfriends!" Jessica nudged Thunderhead as Bets and Anasazi took off right behind her down the trail of packed dirt.

"Look out for wild varmints!" Buck yelled after us.

"Coming, Moon?" Bets winked slyly and threw up her arm over her head like she was directing a round-up.

"Don't gallop!" I yelled after them. "Yet, anyway!"

I nudged Miss Molly with the heels of my tennis shoes, and she surprised me by trotting off right behind them.

I saw a flash of color ahead as someone or something disappeared into the bushes. "What was that?" I asked pointing toward the quivering thicket.

Bets looked toward the shrubs on the trail. "I don't see anything."

Jessica shrugged her shoulders. "Probably just a jackrabbit. They grow pretty big in Cactusville." Her eyes grew wide as she smiled.

Bets giggled.

I watched the underbrush as we trotted past—jackrabbit or not, I wanted to be on the lookout for those wild "varmints" Buck had warned us about. Even Indiana Jones had been bushwhacked a few times. I didn't want to be next!

The Meany-Miney Maneuver

Trotting on a horse was wild! I felt my insides rattling around like a jar full of jelly beans. I soon found that it was much easier to gallop. After a few minutes of "Whoa, Miss Molly—okay, now go—wait, whoa!" I relaxed. Miss Molly was either really patient with me or really confused—I wasn't sure which. But I was able to catch up with Bets and Jess, and we headed down the "long trail," as they called it.

Riding a horse wasn't as bad as I had thought. Actually it wasn't as hard as riding my bike. When we came to a hole in the road, Miss Molly galloped right over it. I didn't even feel a bump. My bike would have jolted.

As we rounded the bend through the cottonwood trees, I saw the same flash of color in the shrubs. I turned my head and saw trouble lurking within inches of us. To my dismay, out jumped Elmer and Todd.

"Stick 'em up!" they yelled as they pulled red bandannas up over their chocolate-stained mouths.

I rolled my eyes. "Give me a break!"

"We're here to take yer hosses hostage, you purple-haired freak!" yelled Elmer as he waved a Turbo One Thousand Super Soaker water pistol in my face.

"Oh!" Jessica trembled wildly in her saddle. "Like we're so scared!"

"Petrified!" Bets giggled and pretended to be scared too.

"Hand 'em over, you lily-livered polecats!" Todd aimed his Super Soaker at the dirt and pommeled the ground with a jet stream of dark blue liquid.

"What's in your water pistol, little boy?" Bets asked, pointing at the blue-soaked path.

Elmer laughed wickedly, "Heh-heh-heh! It's ink. And it's aimed right at your pea-pickin' face, Moon Beam!" He growled and pointed his blaster at me. His yellowish eyes glowed like an alley cat's as he snarled. His long, skinny bowlegs were pushed down inside a pair of bright blue cowboy boots.

"Elmer Higgins, you put that thing down right now!" Jessica was getting flustered.

Elmer slowly turned the tip of the blaster toward her and then back at me. "Make me, hombre!"

Bets nudged Anasazi with her heel, and the black horse took a step forward.

"Hold it right there!" Todd pointed his Super Soaker at Bets. "One more move and you're blasted!"

"Why do you need three horses?" I decided to try reasoning—an obvious mistake.

Elmer snickered and said to Todd, "We're gonna skin 'em and sell 'em for cat food!"

Jessica huffed and crossed her arms, still holding the reins in her hand. "You're horrible, Elmer! Now please get out of our way. Buck won't like this at all."

"Oh, Toddie," Elmer made a goofy face, "she said *please*."

Todd spat at the ground. "Buck's gone for the day. I saw his pickup pull away a while ago to get supplies," he snarled. "So we're in charge now!"

"Well, I guess there's only one thing to do, Bets." Jessica winked.

"What?" Bets' eyebrows wrinkled as she looked at Jessica, who smiled knowingly. "Ohhh!" Bets nodded and gave Jessica a thumbs-up. "You mean . . ."

They yelled together, their voices almost squealing, "the Meany-Miney Maneuver!"

"What?" Elmer and Todd looked at one another, confused.

Jess and Bets took a deep breath and called out at the same time, "Meany! Miney! Hup!"

At once, Thunderhead and Anasazi reared up in the air at the same time and whinnied with all the fury of Silver, the Lone Ranger's horse. It was awesome!

"Look out!" Elmer screamed. He and Todd backed away, pumping their guns and squirting with all their might.

Suddenly Elmer's foot caught a tree root and he crashed into Todd. As they fell to the ground in fright, two fountains of blue ink shot into the air! One in Elmer's direction and one in Todd's! Elmer and Todd drenched each other from head to foot in the blue stuff.

"Giddyap!" Jessica yelled. So did Bets. Their horses thundered off down the path.

"Giddyap!" I yelled. I punched Miss Molly and then grabbed the horn, holding on for dear life! Down the trail we flew, our hair streaming behind us. We laughed hysterically!

I glanced back quickly. There were Elmer and Todd rolling around kicking and screaming like two giant blueberries on the path. The Meany-Miney Maneuver had worked!

The Super-Stupendous Plan

"Y ee-hah!" Bets hollered as we rounded a trail.

"Whoopie!" Jess shouted after her.

"Hold on, guys!" I laughed and gripped the saddle horn as Miss Molly galloped close behind.

"Could you believe Elmer and Todd could be so loony?" Jess giggled.

All through the wooded trail, the sound of snickering and giggling could be heard. Bets, Jessica, and I laughed so hard our stomachs hurt.

The rest of the day went great! We rode down to a stream and watered the horses. Boy, were they thirsty! I tied Miss Molly's reins to a tree branch and stretched out on the grass by the water to watch a small army of ants.

"So how did you two get Thunderhead and Anasazi to do the Mealymouthed whatchamacallit?"

"The Meany-Miney Maneuver?" Jessica smiled.

Bets jumped off Anasazi and sat down beside us. "Should we tell her, Jess?"

"Well . . ." she looked at me long and hard. "Maybe, if you promise not to tell."

I was impatient. "I promise already, so tell me!"

"We made it up, sort of," said Jessica. "See, Buck had trained these two horses to rear up for a rodeo trick. He taught them to do it every time they heard the command, 'Hup!' When we found *that* out, we didn't want everyone to know about it, so we added the Meany-Miney business."

"Oh!" I finally understood. "So they're really jumping up for the 'Hup' part."

"Exactly!" Bets said.

"That's cool," I said. "Now, does anybody have any ideas yet about how I could raise money to buy my own pony?"

"You still want to buy one, Moon?" Bets flicked her long hair over her shoulder and sat down beside me.

"I really do. Especially after today. Have you ever heard of the Pony of the Americas? It's a gorgeous breed!"

"I have," said Bets. "Those are the ponies with the long name."

Jessica nodded. "Yeah, I've heard of them. They have those spots on them sort of like the Appaloosa."

I pulled the clipping out of my pocket and showed it to them. "Look at this beauty!"

"Let me see!" Bets took the clipping while Jess looked over her shoulder.

"It says that the Pony of the Americas, commonly called the POA, is something new," Jessica read. "It is the perfect size for an older kid—like you, Moon! It is a cross between the Arabian and the quarter horse."

"Good stock," added Bets. Bets was so smart.

"It is trimmed and ridden western style, which means," Jessica explained, "that's how they give him a haircut for his tail and mane." She continued, "The Pony of the Americas is never shown in the stretched stance."

"What does that mean?" I asked.

"Well," Bets said, "when you train a horse for show—you know, like competition—you sometimes have them stretch out their legs to make them look more flashy."

"So," I figured, "the POA just stands there kind of normal-like then?"

Jessica nodded. "I guess."

"Do you think Buck could help me find one of those POA kind of ponies?" I asked.

"I'm sure he could *find* you one, Moon." Bets twisted up her mouth like she was thinking. "But how are you going to pay for it?"

"I could sell something," I said. "I once sold greeting cards to buy a bicycle. But that wouldn't be enough to buy a pony."

"Well, my aunt raises hot peppers and makes a special hot sauce with them," Jessica said brightly. "She calls it her 'secret recipe'."

"Hot peppers! Yuk! People eat those?" I made a face.

"Sure! They're a hot item around here, if you know what I mean," Jessica wiggled her eyebrows.

Bets giggled. "People eat them by the gallons here in Cactusville." She stretched out her arms vertically.

"First you grow them," Jessica said, tapping her finger. "Then you pick them and can them in glass jars. Bets and I could help you. There are a lot of different recipes. We could put them all together and make our own gourmet hot peppers!" I could almost see the wheels spinning in Jessica's mind.

"Hmm," I pondered. "Hot peppers . . . let's do it!"

Honesty Is the Best Way

Finding a place to grow red-hot peppers was a problem. My
mother wasn't too keen on the idea of me digging up part of
her yard just to grow hot peppers. And I wasn't exactly honest
with her about the reason why.

"You have to tell her, Moon. Honesty is the best way." Bets
stood with her hands on her hips, looking at me, and so did
Jessica. How anyone could be so totally honest was beyond me!

"I'll tell her before I plant them!" I tried to use my puppy-
dog eyes on them. "Even if I do, she isn't going to let me dig up
the whole backyard so I can grow peppers."

"Hey! What about that field behind your uncle and aunt's
house?" Bets asked Jessica.

"What? You mean that old lettuce field?" Jessica said.

Bets was insistent. "Yeah, or any field. Doesn't your uncle
have a bunch of fields?"

"No, he sold them on account of he and Aunt Bert were getting too old to farm anymore. They sold everything except that
old field behind their house. But that's probably where Aunt
Bert grows them—red-hot peppers, that is."

"Do you think your aunt would let me use it to grow my
own peppers?" I asked.

"I could ask. You never know." Jessica bent up her arms and held her palms out.

The next day I heard the doorbell ring and there was Jessica standing on my doorstep with a big, brown, paper bag in her hands.

"What's that, Jess?" I asked, pointing to the sack.

"Well . . ." Jessica poked at different things in the sack. "Just a few things, like gardening gloves, a spade, some clippers . . ."

"For what?" I asked.

"For you, Moon!" She held the sack out to me.

"For me?" I couldn't believe it.

"Yep! Aunt Bert had them sitting out in her barn. She's tired of hot peppers. Wants to try her hand at cross-stitch."

My eyes squinted. "Your aunt's name is Bert?"

"Short for Bertha," Jessica said casually.

"What about the field? Can I use it?" I whispered because I still hadn't gotten around to sharing my little scheme with Mom.

"She said it was okay. We have to promise to be good farmers and take care of the plants." Jessica shook her finger at me in warning.

"The plants?"

"Yeah, normally you have to start them from seed back around February or March. My aunt's already got a half acre of the things planted! If we'll fertilize them and keep them watered, she'll let you have all you want!"

"Wow! When can I pick them?"

"They'll be ripe in about a week. Do you think you can wait that long?"

"For my pony? I can wait as long as it takes. Did she tell you how to cook them and all that stuff?"

"Well, she keeps her canning stuff all out by the barn. It's kind of like a little patio she's fixed up. She calls it her work spot. She said all that canning made her house too hot, so she keeps a little cook stove out there. But there's one thing I need to tell you."

"What's that?"

"She wouldn't give me her secret recipe. You see, she wins all these ribbons at the county fair, and she says that if it ever got out, then everyone would be making it and it wouldn't be a secret recipe anymore."

"Nuts!" I snapped my fingers. "If we could just get our hands on that secret recipe . . . why, I'd sell so many jars of red-hot peppers that I could buy two ponies!"

"Oh, well." Jessica shrugged her shoulders. "We could just look one up in a recipe book. Hot peppers are hot peppers, right?"

I nodded, but my mind was already racing. How could I come up with a way to get my hands on that secret recipe? If Hubie were here, I'll bet he'd have a plan in the shake of a stick. I decided to keep that thought to myself since Jessica and Bets seemed to be so touchy about this total honesty thing.

But the red-hot peppers were mine! "Yippee!" I cupped my hand over my mouth and stepped outside to close the door behind me. "Pony of the Americas, here I come!"

Jessica laughed. "I thought you might be excited. Say, the garden's not far from here. You want to grab your bike and go look at it? It needs a little work."

"Sure, let's go!" I yelled back into the house, "Mom, I'm going to ride my bike."

We rode past Bets' house, and she jumped on her bike and came with us. Jessica was right. It only took a few minutes to get there. Now if I could only get a hot pepper sauce recipe that fast . . .

The Secret Red-Hot Pepper Plantation

Aunt Bert's place was really neat. There were trees all over her yard, with rose gardens on the side. We walked past the big row of trees in the back to the patio Jessica had told me about.

Aunt Bert's work spot was perfect. It had a big pot called a pressure cooker with an instruction book that told us about canning food. We checked it out and then walked down a path to the garden.

"Whoa!" I slapped my hand to the side of my face. "Look, girlfriends, it's not just a garden . . . It's a whopping plantation!"

Jess and Bets laughed at me. But they didn't realize that if you grew up in L.A., the closest you might come to a garden was potted plants. Mrs. Pockburton—a neighbor two doors away—had liked to talk to her potted plants. And who wanted to visit for long with a lady who spends her day chatting with a bromeliad? Not Moon Holly Soileau . . . that's for sure!

I looked down at the rows and rows of pepper plants. They stood knee high. Popping out all over the leafy plants were

bright green peppers—my own secret plantation! Hubie
Hoffmeister couldn't have planned it better himself! But all
around the rows were bunches and bunches of weeds. We bent
over and started pulling some of them. They squeaked through
my fingers like licorice-whips on hot pavement. After only a
few minutes my body was hot and sweaty, my back was starting to hurt, and my knuckles were numb.

"Hey, Jess, do you think Aunt Bert always had to come out
here and pull all these weeds? I mean, seeing how she's getting
old and everything, it seems like she'd keel over or something."

"No, she has a tractor, and she usually dragged this
machine-thingy around that puts a lot of weed killer on the
dirt. But we don't have any money to buy that, right?" Jess
kept pulling and tossing.

"No." I was trying to *make* money, not spend it. I looked
toward the barn. "Can we look in the barn and see if there are
any tools to dig up some of this stuff?"

"I guess it's okay, Moon." Jessica looked back at Aunt Bert's
house. "Let's go look." She took off for the barn with Bets and
me right behind her.

Nosing around in the barn loft reminded me of the movies
where the girl would be poking around in the attic of an old
house and she'd stumble upon a long-lost family treasure. So I
made up this big story and told Jess and Bets about it. My
eyes got really big as I explained it.

"Finding out that the heirloom was worth a fortune, she suddenly found herself richer than a game-show contestant! Maybe
we'll find a treasure, or better yet, Aunt Bert's secret recipe!"

"Forget the recipe, Moon." Jessica shook her finger at me
again. "If Aunt Bert wanted us to have it, she'd give it to us."

I just smiled as I pulled a cardboard box away from the
wall. "Hey, look!" The girls came and peeked over my shoulder

at the weird contraption I had discovered. It was made of old, grayed wood and had a metal thing at the bottom that was rounded on the sides and had a point at the end.

"Oh, I know what it is," said Jessica. "It's an old plow. My grandpa used it to make the rows in his garden in the old days."

I snapped my fingers. "I have an idea! Let's get some of that rope over there"—I pointed to a coil of rope hanging on a nail— "and tie the plow, to my waist. You two can push the plow and I can pull it. We'll dig up those weeds in no time flat!"

"Gee," Jessica said crossing her arms, "I don't know if that'll work."

"Sure it will!" I was brilliant and I knew it.

"Look!" Bets pointed. "Fertilizer!" A big burlap sack of grainy mixture sat close to the attic railing. The words across it read "Farmer Farkle's Famous Fertilizer."

"Let's take that stuff and use it," Bets suggested.

So we borrowed the plow and the Farkle fertilizer. I ran a big rope through the plow, and Jess and I hoisted it down to Bets, who waited below. Then I used the same rope to tie it to the top of the grain sack and lower it with a squeaky, old pulley that hung above my head from the rafters.

With the help of a rusty wheelbarrow, we heaved and grunted and finally lugged all the stuff out to the side of the garden. I stopped to catch my breath. This gardening business was a lot of work! Finally I got up and dropped the plow right in front of a big patch of weeds. After hitching myself up to it, Jessica and Bets took turns pushing the plow while I tried to pull. Slowly but surely, the weeds started coming up.

As I grunted my way toward the end of the first row, my eyes fell on two sinister pairs of sneakers. I slowly glanced up in dismay to find two sneaky snoops had discovered us. "What do *you* want?" My lip curled in a disgusted frown.

Karate Moon

Well, if it isn't a real, genu-ine donkey!" I heard a familiar, sarcastic voice say. There stood Elmer Higgins with his arm resting on Todd Tweetweiler's shoulder. Elmer glared at me and I glared back.

"Who invited you, Elmer?" I stopped and wiped the sweat from my face.

"Oh, look, Todd. It's a talking donkey . . . with purple hair! It must be a freak donkey, like in the circus."

Todd started making "hee-haw" noises. He held his fingers up over his head and wiggled them like mule's ears.

I probably did look a little silly, standing there with a plow hitched to my waist, but I certainly wasn't going to let Elmer Higgins get the best of me. "How'd you ever get all the ink out of your hair, blueberry head? Did your mommy help you wash it out?"

"What's it to you, Moon Beam?"

"Uh, guys, we're a little busy and it's hot out here, so if you don't mind . . ." Jessica tried to sound nice, as always.

"What're you doing?" Elmer propped his foot up on the open bag of fertilizer.

"Get your foot off, mushbrain! That's my future you got

your big, hairy, size twelves propped up on!" I *didn't* try to sound nice, as usual.

"What?" He made an innocent face. "You mean this . . . ?" He kicked at the bag. "This little bag? Whoops!" He smiled as the bag tumbled over. "I guess I did a boo-boo."

Out spilled Farmer Farkle's Famous Fertilizer granules! They poured onto a patch of dandelions.

That was all that I could take! I tore at the rope around my waist and tossed it to the side. Never had anyone made me as mad as Elmer did that day. I kicked at a dirt clod in my path, and it disintegrated. At long last, Elmer Higgins would suffer the wrath of Moon Beam!

Todd's eyes grew wide as he looked at Elmer. Jessica and Bets looked at me.

"No, Moon. It's not worth it." Bets tugged at my arm.

"He deserves it, Bets!" I whispered, but never took my steely-eyed stare away from Elmer.

"A lot of people deserve a lot of things, Moon. But it's not our place to give it to them," Jessica whispered on the other side of me as she pulled on my other arm.

Staring straight ahead, I continued walking toward Elmer as I drew my fingers together tightly and held my hands up in one of those karate stances I had learned. I would surprise him with a sensational move and whack the daylights out of him. It would be the fight of the century! I felt like the Karate Kid!

Elmer pulled his fists up in front of his face. "I'm gonna flatten you, Moon Beam!"

"You're not supposed to hit girls!" Jessica yelled at him.

"She's asking for it! Aren't you, Moon Beam?"

"Stop it, both of you!" Bets pleaded.

At the same time, Elmer and I drew our arms back, elbows bent, and charged toward each other.

"You're mincemeat, Moon Beam!" he roared.

"Bite the dust, dirtball!" I whooped.

Then, just as I could see those yellowish eyes coming at me, glowing like a maimed firefly, it happened. Bets jumped in front of me, right in the path of Elmer Fudd Higgins—her hands in front of her face, her eyes shut tight, ready to take the blow that was meant for me!

"Move it or lose it!" He kept charging.

"*Enough!*"

The dry Cactusville air grew quiet. We looked up. There was Todd Tweetweiler standing in front of Bets with his arms sticking out, flailing all over the place like he was going to take the hit himself.

"Are you nutso, Tweetweiler?" Elmer stuck his finger in Todd's chest.

"I can't let you do it, Elmer." Todd closed his eyes, ready to take whatever it was that was coming.

"Todd, this is between me and Moon Beam. Besides, you're supposed to be on my side. What gives?"

"It's Bets, Elmer. When I saw her standing there like she was all ready to get hit on account of Moon, I just couldn't take it. I felt sorry for her." Todd was still holding his eyes shut.

Now it was Elmer who was kicking at the dirt clods. "I just can't believe it!" He swung at the ground with his foot. "You're turning yellow, Todd!"

He took another swing with his other foot, but this time it stuck right in a hole—an old mole tunnel—and *whoosh!* Down went his ankle and stayed right there. Elmer grabbed his calf with one grimy hand and dug frantically at the ground. With the other hand he searched for the top of the giant, high-top sneakers his mother had probably paid many buckaroos for.

"H-help me, somebody!" Elmer's voice sounded funny, not ferocious like it had a few minutes before. "I -I'm not kidding, guys. My shoe is stuck! I can't get it out!"

His eyes grew wide and his nose scrunched up and down, making his big ears wiggle. He looked for all the world like a trapped rat.

It was too perfect! Like a desert hyena, I started laughing. "Well, if that isn't funny I don't know what is!" I fell backward on the grass and rolled. Then Bets and Jessica stepped forward.

"We'll help you, Elmer." Jessica's face was serious. I couldn't believe it! This was Elmer Higgins they wanted to help. The guy who wanted to flatten me, and douse us all in blue ink. Now they wanted to help him?

"Wait, girlfriends." I tried to get up. "Let him stay there a while. We'll go have lunch and maybe come back later and get him out. It'll teach him a lesson," I pleaded, but they didn't listen.

"Come on, Elmer!" Bets dug at the hole around his sneaker.

"Here, I'll pull on his foot, and you pull that mound of dirt away, Bets," Jessica told her.

So Elmer yanked, Jessica pulled, and Bets dug. Soon the dirt-covered sneaker was freed, and Bets got busy filling up the hole again with dirt. Elmer sprawled back on the ground trying to catch his breath.

"My mother would have killed me if I had come home without that sneaker!"

"Well, now you'll just have to explain a little dirt," Jessica said.

Todd's blue eyes glanced at Jessica and Bets and then back at Elmer. "Do you have something to say, Elmer?"

Elmer got quiet for a minute, then he sat forward. At first crouching like a cat he jumped up in the air and kicked his feet to the side. "Yeah!" he yelled. "You better watch your back, Moon Beam! I'll be back! And next time—you'll be mincemeat!"

Then he took off on his bike, disappeared around the house, and tore down the street. Todd sighed and lumbered over to jump on his own bike. With sheepish-looking eyes, he followed Elmer.

"I knew it!" I pounded the ground. "You can't be nice to people like that, you guys!"

"It doesn't matter. We have to keep trying." Bets looked at me with her dark brown eyes.

"But why?" I asked. "Why are you so nice, especially to people like Elmer Higgins?"

Bets and Jessica smiled at one another and then looked at me. "Oh, that . . . We've been meaning to tell you."

I shook my head and held up my hands. "What? What is it?"

A Little Tug-of-Heart

So what's the deal?" I asked Bets and Jessica, who stood smiling at me with their arms crossed. "Is it a big secret like your aunt's recipe?"

"Oh, it's no secret!" Jessica answered slyly.

"But you have to promise to listen, Moon." Bets crossed her heart.

Boy! I thought to myself. They sure look sneaky. "Okay," I answered. "Go ahead—I'll listen. I promise. Cross my heart."

"It's like this," Jessica began. "First we had to get cleaned up from the inside out. Then our hearts began to change."

"Oh!" I said sarcastically. "Now I understand perfectly!"

"Now, Moon!" Bets shook her finger at me. "You promised to listen."

"Okay, already!" I surrendered.

"We used to be like you, Moon," Jessica explained. "You know, sneaking around and not being totally honest with our parents. After a while you get to where you don't even feel guilty about lying or being dishonest."

Guilty? I thought. I'm supposed to feel guilty?

"But one of the kids at school handed us a little booklet called a tract. It had a story in it about Jesus Christ's love for us."

"Jesus Christ?" I said. "I've heard of him—really, I have."

"Yeah, Moon," Bets explained. "It's one thing to hear about Jesus, but it's another to know him—personally!"

It was then that I got this funny little feeling inside of me that was hard to explain. Kind of like a little string inside of me was being tugged on. "You mean like a friend?"

"You got it!" Bets looked sort of excited for some reason.

"But how could that be?" I felt confused. "Jesus is hidden behind the clouds or something, right?"

Jessica spread her arms out wide. "Jesus is God and God is everywhere! He can speak to us through the Bible. And as we get to know him, he speaks to us in other ways. But Jesus doesn't stay where he's not invited. You have to invite him to be your friend."

"Now wait a pea-picking minute!" I stopped Jessica. "My friend Hubie Hoffmeister says religion's for sissies. He says that I have to make my own way in this world and that nothing comes easy."

"Well," Bets agreed, "I guess part of that is true. Life isn't always easy. Just when it seems we're having a good day, here comes Elmer Higgins!"

"But instead of throwing up your fists, Moon," Jessica added, "what if you learned to see Elmer in a different way? Maybe he feels bad inside and doesn't know how to tell us."

This conversation was going somewhere, but I wasn't sure where. "But what about *my* feelings?" I wanted to know.

"Well, if we all just cared about 'making our own way,' as your friend Hubie said, then wouldn't the world just be in a big mess?"

"It is in a big mess!" I blurted. "How would you like to live without a dad?" Oh, no! I thought. I felt a dumb tear falling down my cheek. I wiped it angrily. Dad had left a long time ago. He and Mom didn't see eye to eye, but Mom and I had decided to be grown-ups about it. "Look!" I shouted at Bets and Jessica, "I don't need it! I can do it on my own. Really, I can!"

"Jesus loves you, Moon." Bets tried to wipe my face.

"Stop it!" I stood and ran for my bicycle. I was feeling weird inside, like all I wanted to do was cry. But this wasn't a play, and I wasn't selling any tickets!

"We love you too, Moon!" Jessica yelled after me.

I stopped dead in my tracks. They both loved me and I knew it. They really loved *me*, Moon Holly Soileau, just the way I was. Bad temper and all, they loved me! I wanted to run back to them and hug them or something mushy like that, but I kept thinking of Hubie and how goofy he'd think I was acting. So I threw my leg over the seat of my bike to peddle away. "It's okay." I tried to sound normal again. "I'm fine, really, and I'll see you both later."

Only I wasn't going home.

The Secret Recipe Thief

I rode around the house and cut back through the rose garden, being careful not to bump Aunt Bert's bushes. Hiding behind a big tree, I waited until I saw Jessica and Bets pull away. Then I rode down to the work spot to check it out.

Aunt Bert had fixed up a great place to can hot peppers. On the outdoor patio was a cook stove with a blue tarp over the top in case it rained. On top of the cook stove was the biggest pot I'd ever seen. It had a giant lid with a funny-looking compass on the top. Sitting next to the stove was a table with a jar full of cooking utensils and a couple of recipe files. What? *Recipe files*? I hadn't noticed that before. That temptation was too great to resist.

Looking around real casual-like, I reached for the first file. It had a piece of tape around it with writing that read "Specialties." I fumbled through the index, but all I found were recipes for things like Arizona Fried Beef Liver and Squash and Onion Surprise. Yuk!

Then I picked up the other file box—a blue one marked "Aunt Bert's Concoctions." Now that's the ticket!

"Let's see—Apple Pie—Boysenberry Jelly—no, farther back—Radish Delight—ah!" My eyes lit up with delight. Hubie

would be so proud of me! "Aunt Bert's Red-Hot Pepper Recipe!"
I pulled the card out real sneaky-like and looked around to see
if anyone was watching. Then a thought struck my brain. Why
would Aunt Bert leave her "secret recipe" out here in the open
like this? Maybe she was planning on using it just one more
time and would be coming back in a few minutes to look for it.
I had better work fast!

Grabbing a piece of paper and a pencil from her work
table, I scribbled down the ingredients as fast as I could and
stuffed it into my pocket. Then I slipped the recipe card back
into the box. I could get the directions later.

Sure enough! I heard the back door to the house slam shut.
I closed the recipe box just in time. Along came Aunt Bert in
the flesh, ambling across the backyard like a mother elephant.
She stopped to wipe her hands on her apron and then looked
down at me with ice blue eyes. She was a heavy woman with
a red face, and her hair was all tied up on her head in a
flowery scarf.

"Who might you be?" She didn't smile.

I stuck out my hand and gave her the ol' "Hoffmeister
hello." That's what Hubie would call it when he met people for
the first time. He'd smile from ear to ear, look them straight in
the eye, and shake the daylights out of their hand.

"Why, hello, Aunt Bert! If I may call you Aunt Bert, that
is. It's a pleasure to meet you. Moon Holly's the name, and I
am the good friend of your wonderful niece, Jessica! If I may
say so, your lovely niece certainly resembles you in a remark-
able way!"

Aunt Bert seemed to stare straight at me in a kind of stu-
por. She didn't say anything right away. Maybe I had overdone
it a bit. Then I thought, what if she saw me steal her recipe?
Horror of horrors!

Suddenly a thin smile crept across her plump face. "Why thank you . . . Moon Holly, is it?"

"Yes!" I was fast. "Moon Holly is right-o, and you're obviously a woman of high intelligence." Whoops! Too much! The funny look stretched across her face again, and then, suddenly, for some reason she started laughing. I don't know why, but first it was just a chuckle and then she just hauled off and slapped her knee and hooted!

"You're a funny kid, Moon Holly! Jessica told me you're a little different, and she was right!"

Now I had stopped laughing. Different? I may be a little creative, a bit gifted and talented . . . but different? "Great! That's all I need!" I crossed my arms over my chest.

"Is there something I could help you with, Moon?" She rested her arms on her stomach.

"I . . . uh . . . I'm investigating. I might want to write a report this year when school starts," I stalled.

"Oh?"

"Now, you take that big pot up there on the stove . . ."

Aunt Bert pointed to the big pot. "The pressure cooker?"

"Whatever you call it." I kept talking. "You could probably cook a lot of stuff in there, huh?"

Aunt Bert nodded. "Sure, green beans, tomatoes, soup, my famous red-hot pepper sauce . . ." She beamed proudly.

"It's not your average pot," I said. "You could feed a lot of people with it if you wanted. Right?" I continued my speech with the flair of a vacuum cleaner salesperson.

"The idea is to cook enough to store some away for later."

"Sure!" I agreed. "Make a lot. Keep it for later."

She tapped her finger impatiently against her face.

"I guess that's all for now, Aunt Bert. Thanks for your help." I smiled sheepishly.

"Well, it was nice to meet you." Aunt Bert patted the top of my head. "Don't forget to water those pepper plants before you leave. The water hoses are in the shed."

"Sure thing! Thanks a bunch!" I grinned, grateful she was leaving.

"When you get ready to pickle those red-hot peppers, let me know. I'll need to help you with the cooking equipment." She reached to snatch up her recipe boxes and, hefting them up under her thick arm, turned to waddle back toward her kitchen door.

I gulped. "Help with the cooking?"

"Sure. Those aren't toys over there, you know. You shouldn't be using the pressure cooker alone. If you use it the wrong way you could have a mess on your hands."

I hadn't counted on that kind of thing happening. Now how in the world could I use her secret recipe if she was standing over me helping? I would have to give this situation some more thought.

As I stood there scratching my chin and thinking, what did my eyes fall on but that little book on the cart that stood next to the cook stove. I bent over and snatched it up. It was called *Home Canning: A How-To Manual*. The cover was stained and ragged, and the book looked as old as my Great-grandpa Graves. But I opened it up, and it had everything in it that I needed to know about canning vegetables, including how to work the pressure cooker.

Stuffing the book inside my shirt, I hopped on my faithful old bike—that was soon to be replaced with my very own pony—and I headed down the happy trail to my house.

That night, before I went to sleep, I studied the manual for a few minutes to decide how I might cook those peppers all by myself. The book didn't say anything about red-hot peppers, but Aunt Bert had said she used the cooker to make her secret sauce. Cooking her recipe couldn't be much different from the instructions I found for cooking plain old tomatoes. Vegetables were vegetables.

The manual had a bunch of different steps for canning and the last page was missing, but I felt sure that I could handle this project all alone.

Then I felt that funny little "tug" again, and I remembered what Bets and Jessica had said to me about Jesus and all that stuff. I figured the girls probably wouldn't be too happy with me if they knew I stole the recipe. But things were going to turn out super-stupendous! I'd show them! Not everyone was the same, I tried to tell myself. Everyone had to find their own way in this world. Hubie was right.

My mind was jumbled with schemes and ideas. I nodded off to sleep as visions of red-hot peppers danced in my head.

Moon's Marvelous Mush

When I awoke, the sun was just beginning to peek through my window, making the sky all pink and pretty. The manual was still lying across my tummy, and I remembered the garden. Why, I could go over first thing this morning and water the plants and be done with my work for the whole day.

Mom was still asleep, so I left her a note and headed up the street. When I arrived at the garden, I took the hoses that Aunt Bert had given us and set them out with the sprinklers on them so the plants would get saturated with water.

Then I decided to find a spot under a shade tree and take myself a little catnap.

But when I turned around what did I see but the Farmer Farkle's Fertilizer still dumped over. I had forgotten to clean it up after "Fuddsville" had ruined it all. Running over to pick up the sack, I stopped dead in my tracks! The dandelions! They were huge! It must have happened overnight!

I grabbed the sack of fertilizer and read the instructions on the back. They said to use a few tablespoons per plant. So those dandelions had gotten an overdose from "the Farmer" himself! I sat down and tried to pick a few of the dandelions, which were as tall as my waist. I could enter those monster plants in the book of world records. No! Wait a minute! I had a brilliant idea. What if I took the Farmer Farkle's and over-dosed a bunch of the pepper plants? Why, I'd have the biggest and best red-hot peppers in the whole wide world!

I decided to work fast, so I turned off the sprinklers and ran and got a shovel. If a couple of tablespoons would help them grow a little, then a whole shovelful would make them gigantic. Plant by plant I zapped as many as I could with the Farkle mixture.

When I was finished, I turned the sprinklers back on and found a place to sit under a tree and read some more of that manual.

"Oh, me!" I yawned. Maybe a little shut-eye would do me some good. Though I didn't mean to, I fell asleep for three hours! When I awoke, I realized that I had left the sprinklers on. I ran to turn them off before Aunt Bert's backyard became an ocean. Sure enough, the garden was saturated.

I blinked my eyes twice, sure that I was seeing things. "No way! It can't be! Can Farmer Farkle's work that fast? Why, the plants are taller than my head, and look at the peppers!" They were each as big as my two fists—and ripe! Wow!

If I got that cooker going real fast, I could get the secret recipe and whip up the best red-hot pepper sauce in all of Arizona . . . maybe the world!

Picking the peppers was no easy task. I had to tug forever just to pull one of those giant peppers off the vine. But what a crop! I picked as many as I could tote in the wheelbarrow over to the work spot and then went back for more. Hubie's eyes would pop right out of his head if he could see these babies, I thought!

After reading the directions again, I mixed up a batch of the secret sauce right inside the pressure cooker. Whoo, did it smell! No wonder Aunt Bert did all the cooking outside!

I boiled the mixture for a while until I heard something inside the pot go "ping!" Peeking carefully inside, I watched in amazement as the peppers ricocheted off the inside of the pot like ducks in a shooting gallery. Does this mean they're ready? I wondered.

With a huge spoon I began scooping the sauce into a few of the clean jars Aunt Bert had left for us in a box. Then I screwed the lids down tight.

When I had a dozen jars ready I toted them over and put them in the knapsack of my bicycle. I could always come back and finish filling the rest of the jars later, but I just had to see if they would sell. I thought for a moment. *The park*! A lot of people would be at the park today.

As I neared the city park, I could see a few moms starting to arrive with their toddlers. A nursery school class was there too. "Well, there's no time like the present," as you-know-who would say.

A big picnic table sat under a shade tree, and I parked my bike right next to it. After I had arranged the jars of sauce on one end of the table, I climbed onto the tabletop and cleared my throat real loud to hack out all the morning grunge.

I waved my right arm in the air. Then cupping my left hand over my mouth I hollered, "COME AND GET IT! RIGHT HERE TODAY FOR THE FIRST TIME IN CACTUSVILLE, FOLKS, IT'S 'MOON'S MARVELOUS MUSH'! YES, IF YOU LIKE RED-HOT PEPPERS, YOU MUST TRY THESE BABIES! SI-EN-TIH-FE-KALLY RAISED TO MONSTROUS PRO-POR-SHUNS ARE GAH-RON-TEED *THE* BEST . . . *THE* HOTTEST . . . *THE* MOST FAMOUS RED-HOT PEP-PERS IN THE *WHOLE . . . WIDE . . . WORLD*!

I could see heads bobbing up all over the park. Babies were hanging out of their strollers, toddlers were dropping their pails in the sand, and moms were . . . yes! Reaching for their wallets and heading my way! I kept hollering, and waving, and jumping up and down on the picnic table.

Within seconds, a group of ladies had formed around the table saying things like "Have you heard of it, Mildred?" and "It sounds just ma-arvelous!"

"I want some, little girl!" A woman shook a dollar bill at me. "How much?"

Gee, I hadn't thought about that. "It's only . . . six dollars . . . yes . . . six dollars a jar!"

A few of the women looked at one another and shook their heads.

"But!" I quickly held up a finger. "For a special in-tro-duck-tory price today, I will sell the first dozen jars for only four dollars apiece. Now that's a bargain, ladies!" I waited.

"I want one!" yelled a lady in purple jogging pants.

"Give me two!" shouted another.

"Don't be greedy, Alice!" another elbowed her way in.

"Not to worry, ladies," I assured them. "There will be more where these came from! I'll be back later today. You can bank on it!" I felt so smooth. I would have given anything to have my own light-up jacket at this point. But I'd have to figure out my sales strategies later. I had a lot of work to do when I got back to Aunt Bert's place.

It wouldn't be long now, Pony of the Americas. Gee-willikers! Maybe I could buy a whole ranch!

The ladies all started opening their jars of Moon's Marvelous Mush and reaching in with their fingers. I kind of wondered what it must taste like myself, but I hated peppers almost as badly as I hated liver. Gross!

"Ooh!" one mother with a pudgy baby crooned. "It's absolutely delicious!"

"No," said her friend, "it's ma-arvelous!" Then they all giggled and sat down to eat it right then and there.

"Sixty-two, sixty-three," I said counting the money. "Sixty-four dollars!" After I paid back Aunt Bert for the jars, I would make over sixty dollars for myself. Boy, this was going to be easier money than a magazine layout job!

Just as I was about to jump on my bike and start back, I saw the lady in purple jogging pants get a funny look on her face. She had eaten nearly the whole jar of the mush. I watched as she suddenly pulled off one jogging shoe and tossed it. Then she grabbed her foot and started fanning it and hollering to beat all! "My foot!" Leaping up, she started hopping around on her other foot like a kangaroo!

The lady with the pudgy baby and her friend started doing the same thing. Pretty soon, all the women were whooping and hollering and hopping around fanning their feet.

"YEOW!" one yelled. "My foot feels like it's on fire!"

"What?" I couldn't believe my eyes! The park was suddenly full of out-of-their-mind grown-ups doing the wildest jig you've ever seen. Even Los Angeles wasn't this weird!

"It's those peppers!" one screamed. "They've given us all the hot-foot!"

No way, I thought! I ran and grabbed a half-eaten jar of mush. Could it be possible? Then I remembered the Farmer Farkle's. The problem hit me like a ton of bricks. Not only did the extra fertilizer make giant hot peppers . . . it made them fiery! Put that fact together with Aunt Bert's secret recipe and I had given these ladies the hot-foot!

"Give us our money back!" the ladies demanded.

Suddenly the park was surrounded by police blowing whistles and running toward all the commotion. I had better get out of here and fast!

I jumped on my bike and raced across the gravel path and through a cactus garden, knocking over a clay pot and spooking a flock of pigeons. The police were on foot, but one of them ran and jumped on a motorcycle. I was doomed!

I would have given anything at this moment to be back at the Starlight Talent Agency in my purple hair, pestering Miss Cookie and her coffee mug!

Ahead, I saw a deep ditch with a big, round, metal pipe. Go, Moon, go! I told myself. Maybe I could hide in there until the coast was clear. Speeding over the hump, my bike became airborne and wheelied in the air for a few wild seconds before landing in the ditch. I pushed my bike into the pipe, and I found it fit inside perfectly. So I rolled it to the middle and waited.

"Thought you'd get away, huh, Moon?" a burly voice said from the other end of the pipe.

"Oh, no!" I cringed and saw the "copper" on a motorcycle waiting at the opening. His pale, green eyes were narrow, and his mouth was snarled in a crooked grin.

"I didn't know, officer! Honest, I didn't!" I felt like I would cry. "I was just trying to raise some money to buy my pony!"

"Well," he barked, "there'll be no ponies where they're putting you, Moon Holly! You'll be locked away for a long time!" He laughed, and it echoed through the metal pipe like a cheap horror movie.

"No! It can't be!" I wailed. "No, please, no—"

"Moon?" I heard my mom's voice.

"Help me, Mom! They're going to lock me away—"

"Don't be ridiculous, dear." I heard her chuckle. "You must be having a bad dream."

I sat up in bed like a soldier at attention. Bad dream? My eyes felt all stuck together, so I rubbed them and looked down to find the manual lying on my tummy. My eyes squinted at the sunlight dancing through my window. "What day is it?" I scratched my back.

"Saturday. What were you dreaming about, dear?" She ruffled my hair and smiled.

I waited for a minute, remembering the things Jessica and Bets had said to me. "Uh . . ." Should I tell her? "Oh, Mom," I decided, "you know how loony dreams can be. It was nothing—really!"

She looked at me, her face serious. "Are you sure, Moon?"

I nodded. "Yeah, just a goofy dream."

Down the Drain

Our doorbell rang, and I tried to race ahead of my mom to answer it. "I'll get it!" I yelled, still trying to shake the sleep out of my brain cells.

"Oh, go ahead, then." Mom turned and stepped into the kitchen to mix up some yogurt and bran.

I opened the door, and there stood Jessica and Bets with two of the biggest grins I'd ever seen. "What's up?" I asked, yawning.

"You'll never guess, Moon!" Jessica was waggling her wrists and giggling like a scatterbrain.

"What?" I wanted to know.

"It's that Pony of the Americas you've been talking about, Moon." Bets grabbed my shoulders. "We told Buck at the Agape Stables about you wanting to raise money for a pony. He found a real-live POA! She's down at the stables now!" Bets by now was hopping up and down.

"Moon, wait until you see. She's beautiful," Jessica crooned. "Her eyes are so dreamy!"

"What?" I couldn't believe it. "For me? But why?"

"He likes you, Moon. He even said if your mom agreed, that you could pay him off monthly."

"Said what?" I could feel Mom's breath on my neck and could hear the sound of smacking bran.

I wheeled around and smiled at her. "For . . . riding lessons!" I lied. "Please, Mom," I begged in a soft voice, trying to melt her heart and cover up my scheme.

"Riding lessons?" She bit the bait while Jessica and Bets crossed their arms and looked at me as though they were perturbed.

"Well, you've been so bored since we moved here," Mom said. "I guess you deserve some riding lessons. Sure! Go ahead, dear!" She squeezed my shoulders and turned to go slurp down her yogurt.

Jessica clamped down her hands on her hips and glared at me. "Moon, how could you lie like that to your mom!"

"Shhh!" I stepped outside, still in my Mickey Mouse night-shirt, and closed the door behind me. "Don't be so loud. What are you going to do, Jessica, snitch on me?"

Bets shook her head. "It isn't right, Moon. You need to tell your mother the truth!"

I sighed. Why did I have to make friends with the two biggest Pollyannas this side of the mesas? "What if she won't let me have the pony?"

Bets and Jessica just looked at me.

"No!" I stomped my foot. "I won't tell her! Now wait out here for me while I get dressed!" I turned to reach for the door.

Bets and Jessica looked at each other sadly. "I can't." Bets bit her lip.

Jessica shook her head. "Me neither."

"What?" I felt my temper starting to boil. "You mean you won't help me?"

"We can't." Jessica shrugged her shoulders. "It isn't right, Moon. I guess I'll have to go tell my aunt we can't use her garden."

I could see my plans for a pony slowly going down the drain. "Wait, Jessica! Don't be in such a hurry. I understand what you mean about honesty," I said, even though I really didn't. "Could you wait for one more day? I promise to tell my mom tonight. But let me have some time. Please?" I crossed my fingers behind my back.

Jessica uncrossed her arms. "And you'll really do it, Moon? You'll tell your mom everything?"

I nodded my head quickly, my eyes as big as saucers. "Uh-huh! Sure! I promise!"

The girls smiled and hugged me, making me feel like a genuine Dry Gulch bad guy. I guess this was the first sign of that guilt stuff they were talking about.

"We knew you couldn't do it anyway, Moon," Bets added.

"Well, would you mind if we went over to the stables for just a little while?" I asked rather sheepishly.

"Sure!" they answered at the same time.

"Go get dressed, Moon." Jessica shoved playfully at my shoulder.

I streaked through the house like a rocket. "Mom," I yelled as I tore past her, "I'm going to the stables," which was the absolute truth. "Is that okay with you?"

"Sure, Moon."

I broke all records getting dressed. The thought of buying that pony made me smile, but that yucky feeling inside of me—well, it's sort of hard to describe. Like a pesky bee that won't go away, it poked away at my conscience. Oh, phoo! I tried to tell myself. I'll change my ways . . . once I have my pony! I stepped down onto the front porch steps. Looking up at the clouds, I cleared my throat, feeling sort of miserable. I'll change . . . but when?

Everything that Glitters

The Cactusville Adventure Club was on its way to the stables once again. The bike ride to get there was a blur. All I could think about was seeing the pony.

Buck was in the stalls putting down fresh hay when we rode up.

Jessica yelled and startled him. "Buck! Moon's here! Can she see the pony?"

"Whoa there, cowgirls! You spooked me!" Buck dusted hayseed from his blue jeans. "Hey, little Moon. How's about a ride on your very own pony?"

"Yessir!" I beamed.

Gently taking me by the arm, Buck walked with me over to the stall across from us. "Take a gander in there, missy." He pointed into the stall.

I gazed in and saw the most gorgeous brown eyes I had ever seen. I reached in to stroke the pony's nose. "She's beautiful!" It was definitely love at first sight.

Buck opened the stall door and reached for the pony's bridle. He led her out into the paddock, and I ran my hand over her flank. She was a soft cream color with bright rust splotches. Her coat shone in the sunlight like glitter. She was perfect!

"The man I bought her from already had her broke. But she'll have to get used to you, Moon. Let's toss on a saddle and see how she rides." Buck reached for a saddle that was seated on a sawhorse.

I patted the pony's neck and spoke softly to her while Buck handed me the strap to tighten the saddle around her girth. "Hey, Glitter." It sounded so natural. "Is that your name, girl? Glitter?"

Glitter whinnied loudly and stamped her front right hoof. Bets and Jessica laughed and so did Buck.

"Glitter it is!" exclaimed Buck. "Walk her around the paddock once, Moon."

I took Glitter's reins and did just as Buck had said. She followed behind me like a big puppy dog. "Can I ride her now, Buck?"

"Climb up!" he said grinning.

This time I wasn't nervous at all. I placed my left foot in the stirrup and threw over my right leg like a pro. "Easy, girl." I soothed Glitter when she snorted.

Buck walked over and opened the gate to the paddock. "Take her for a saunter out here, Moon." He pointed to the small arena where Bets and Jessica had been taking their riding lessons.

Nudged by my heel, Glitter trotted through the gate and then broke into a run as we entered the arena. Around the turn we galloped, my French braid bouncing up and down on my neck.

"You're sitting too far back," Buck called to me. "Sit a little more forward."

I leaned forward and began to feel more balanced. Glitter and I were going to get along just great!

My mind kept going back to what Jessica and Bets had said to me. I knew they were just trying to help. But things with me and my mom were different, especially since Dad had left. Mom didn't always understand me and I . . . well, *had* to start lying to make her happy. After all, her happiness was the most important thing, wasn't it?

"Bring her in, Moon!" Buck yelled at me.

Pulling back on the reins, I slowed Glitter to a trot and then brought her to a dead stop right in front of the gate. "Good, girl!" I patted Glitter behind the ears.

"Well, Moon, what does your mom have to say about you getting your first pony?" Buck asked. "Pretty excited, eh?"

I wasn't sure if the girls had told him, but I wasn't in the mood to tell another lie. "Well, Buck, I have to talk to my mother about all of this pony business tonight," I confessed.

The girls smiled up at me while I dismounted from Glitter.

"Sure thing, Moon." He nodded and took the reins. "Let me know something soon."

"I will." I tried to sound hopeful.

Buck walked away with Glitter, but I kept watching until she disappeared into her stall. "She's the most beautiful pony I've ever seen!"

"I hope your mom says yes, Moon." Bets smiled.

"She will!" I decided. Even if I had to . . . *No.* I told myself. No more lies. I would just have to come up with a new plan.

"Say," I said to the girls. "I need to get back and talk to my mom. See you later?"

Bets nodded. "Right!"

"Sure, Moon," Jessica agreed. "We understand."

They understood. But I didn't. How was I going to explain Glitter to Mom?

The Lie that Grew

Worry, worry, worry!" I muttered to myself. I must have ridden my bike in circles for a good half hour around the stables before coming to a decision. I just had to get Mom to say
yes, and the only way seemed to be to prove to her that I could
make the money to pay for Glitter.

I rode back to the house to get the how-to manual. By
myself, I was going make Aunt Bert's secret red-hot pepper
sauce. I was going to *make* it all work out—somehow.

I tiptoed through the house and made my way back to my
bedroom. Sure enough, lying across my rumpled bed was the
manual. I scanned through its pages once again. I wasn't sure
what kind of stuff Aunt Bert needed to make the sauce, so just
to be safe I raided Mom's kitchen. Into a paper bag went vinegar, sugar, an onion, some canned tomatoes, and some spices.
"Moon?" I heard Mom call.

"Ma'am?" I stuffed the sack inside the oven.

Mom walked into the kitchen. "What're you doing?"

"Uh, just trying to find something to nibble on," which
could possibly have been true.

"Well, okay. You can have the rest of the chicken left over
from last night." She reached for the oven knob. "Want me to
heat it up for you?"

"No!" I grabbed the knob and stood in front of the glass, see-through oven door. "I'm not *that* hungry. Thanks anyway, Mom."

She stood staring at me for a minute with a really suspicious look on her face. "Are you up to something, Moon?" she wanted to know.

I shook my head. "Uh, no, ma'am. Really, I'm not!" I was beginning to break into a sweat.

"Okay," she insisted, "out with it! What have you done? Did you fall off that horse today?"

"Oh, no, ma'am!" I couldn't let Glitter take the blame. "I was just wondering if . . . if you would . . . let me go back and ride just one more time today. Please?"

"Well . . ." She thought for a moment. "If you'll go back into your room and make your bed and pick up your dirty socks, I'll let you go back."

I almost leaped into her arms. "Thank you, Mom! I'll do it. I'll clean my whole room!"

"For mercy's sakes, Moon, you would have thought I handed you the golden egg!"

I tore down the hallway to my room, leaving my mom standing there with a really confused look on her face.

I made short work of my room, tucking the sheets under and tossing my socks under the bed. Inside my T-shirt went the manual and . . . Oh, no! The vinegar and stuff! I glanced down the hallway and saw Mom walking into her bedroom with a magazine. I took a few giant steps past her door while calling out, "See you later, Mom!" Then I crept into the kitchen to nab the sack from out of the oven.

"Bye, dear." She munched on an apple. I was gone in a flash.

All the way down the street I rehearsed the steps from Aunt Bert's secret recipe in my mind. First clean the peppers with water; then cook them in the spicy mixture; then put them in the jars. Or was it, put them in the jars first; then add the secret recipe? Oh, well! I'd read it all over again when I got to Aunt Bert's place.

When I got to the garden, I looked around for signs of Aunt Bert or the girls. No one was around. Good! Now to harvest those peppers.

I could see part of my wacky dream was right. On the ground sat the sack of Farmer Farkle's Fertilizer still dumped over on the dandelions. Except the dandelions weren't humongous. They were brown and shriveled. The fertilizer had burned them up! It was a good thing I hadn't shoveled it all over the peppers!

The row of peppers in front of me looked just right for harvesting. The peppers looked plump and red. I sat on the ground pulling peppers from each plant until my fingers hurt. Ouch! Some nasty-looking, crawly bugs kept jumping on me and sticking to my T-shirt. "Go away, you mutant aliens!" I kept zinging them with my fingers, but I didn't stop picking the peppers. Nor did I notice that the manual had slipped onto the ground beside me.

Once I had a big pailful of peppers, I hauled them over to the water spigot and doused them with a ton of water. Then I took each pepper out and wiped it with my T-shirt to be sure it was clean. No one would ever say that Moon's Marvelous Mush had dirty peppers in it.

Stretching out my T-shirt at the bottom, I filled it with the peppers so I wouldn't have to dump them back in that dirty wheelbarrow. I bent my knees and walked carefully over to the work spot. "Okay, down you go!" I said and let go of my shirt so the red-hot peppers would tumble out. Soon the work table was loaded with peppers now all bright and shiny in the sun.

I turned to look at the stove. Looks like a regular stove to me, I thought, shrugging my shoulders. The big pressure cooker was still sitting on top of it. I had made scrambled eggs plenty of times, so turning on the stove would be easy.

The jar full of utensils had a knife in it, which I used to chop up all the peppers and the onion. Ouch! I poked my finger. Next I stood on my tiptoes and poured everything into the cooker—the onion, the tomatoes, the vinegar, the sugar and spices. Best of all, I dumped in every single one of those red-hot peppers. Wow! I stared at the mixture. The pot's filled all the way to the top! My feet started aching. Using the stool that stood underneath the table would be better than standing on my tiptoes, so I pulled it over and climbed up on it.

Whew! All this stuff sure does make my eyes water! I stirred it up with a huge spoon. I wasn't sure what it was supposed to look like, but it seemed to have everything in it. I closed the lid and clamped down the sides just like the book said to do.

After turning up the knob on the stove to "high" so it would cook real fast, I got out the box of jars and lids to count them and rinse them off with the water hose.

I wiped each jar dry with a hand towel and lined them up in six rows. Thirty-six sparkling jars! Plenty to get me started. I did some multiplication. If I did sell each jar at four bucks each, I calculated, why, I'd make a hundred and forty-four buckaroos! That'd prove to Mom I could buy Glitter for sure!

Suddenly the pressure cooker started making a wacky noise. I climbed back up on the stool to take a look. The dial on top was rocking back and forth, and steam was shooting out of the top like a steamboat. Wearing a pot holder glove on each hand, I wrestled with the pot handles. The cooker just kept vibrating, and I didn't know what to do! Oh, no! I felt frantic. Where is that manual?

The Red-Hot Pepper Fiasco

W hen all the world is crazy, don't panic!" Hubie used to say to me.

I took a deep breath and decided to let the sauce boil a little bit longer. What could it hurt? Then I turned off the stove knob.

"Now to take a look at my masterpiece," I giggled.

Just as I was reaching for the lid I heard a voice say, "Hey, Moon Beam! I've been watching you, and that dumb pony of yours is history!"

"Ahrgh!" I growled. It was Elmer and Todd. Again! "How do *you* know about my pony, Fuddster?"

"We've been down to the stables, and we know all about your scheme. When Jessica's aunt finds out what you've been doing, that pony'll be history!"

"By the time she finds out, I'll be finished!" I yanked at the lid with a pot holder in my hand. It seemed to be stuck.

"Oh, look! The karate kid can't even lift the lid off her mush!" Tweetweiler squawked.

I pulled at the lid again, deciding to ignore them.

"What's the matter?" Elmer yapped. "Cat got your whole body, Moon Beam?"

"If you must know, I *can't* get this lid off, and I don't think *anyone* is strong enough to do it!" I stood towering above them on the stool with my hands on my hips, waiting for them to bite the bait.

"You're a weakling! Show her, Elmer!" Todd flexed a scrawny muscle.

"Get out of the way." Elmer, waving a grungy hand at me, pushed his way to the stool. "Girls don't know how to do anything!"

I stepped down to the side of the stool. "No way! You can't get it off!" I half smiled.

First Elmer yanked. Then Todd hammered at it with a stick. Then all three of us grabbed it and wrestled the cooker to the ground.

"Hold it!" Elmer was panting like a hound dog. "Tweetweiler, get me that crowbar over there. I'll get this thing off for good!"

Todd ran and dragged the heavy crowbar over to Elmer.

"Now, all of us together. Heave ho!"

We sat on the crowbar while Elmer held the pot handle.

Suddenly I heard Aunt Bert's croaky voice exclaim, "What in the world?" just as the lid exploded into the air.

Gushing into the skies of Cactusville soared the red-hot mush in a nuclear explosion of red-hot peppers, onions, tomatoes, and vinegar! Marvelous Mush was everywhere! And the force of the lid blasting off sent Elmer, Todd, and me flying in all directions!

Hubie would have said, "Whatever goes up must come down!" because all of us—Elmer, Todd, me, and Aunt Bert— were covered with a shower of red-hot pepper mush!

"Yah!" Todd screamed. "It's hot! And nasty!"

"And stinky! Get it off me!" Elmer wailed. "I'm calling my attorney!"

"You don't have an attorney." Todd looked confused.

"Then I'll get one!" Elmer almost cried.

"Well, I never!" Aunt Bert stomped her foot, and slipping down she crashed to the ground, kicking and wallowing in a pile of nasty red-and-green goo.

Then my worst imaginable nightmare happened. I looked up and saw Jessica and Bets running toward us with none other than . . . my mom! I was doomed!

"Oh, Moon!" my mom shrieked. "What on earth have you done?"

17

Moon Beam Takes a Bath— Inside Out

It certainly took a lot of explaining on my part to Aunt Bert *and* to Jessica and Bets. But worst of all, I had to tell Mom what I had done.

This time I told the truth. It didn't take long to figure out that Jessica and Bets and even Buck had been trying to steer me onto the right trail.

After I was hosed down, I gritted my teeth and forced out a feeble, "I'm sorry!" to Elmer and Todd. There I stood soaking wet and feeling like a great big zero. I had cleaned up on the outside, but inside I still felt grungy.

I was such a dripping mess that Mom didn't even want me in our car. So I promised to ride my bike straight home— and this time I meant it. Although I didn't deserve it, Mom believed me.

Jessica and Bets rode with me. I'll never forget the look on Aunt Bert's face as she stood with tomato dripping off her nose and a big piece of onion sliding down her red cheeks.

"I'm sorry," I told her for the fortieth time. Then I peddled down her driveway behind my two best friends.

"I wouldn't blame you if you didn't want to be my friends anymore, you guys." I shook my head.

"We're still your friends." Jessica smiled. "We just hate to see you learn lessons the hard way."

I swallowed the lump in my throat. "I think I waited too late to realize that friendship is even more important to me than owning a pony."

"We feel the same way about you, Moon." Bets' hair flew around her face.

"Will you forgive me?" I wasn't acting.

"Oh, Moon, we forgive you. Don't you understand?" Jessica smiled her prettiest smile. "That's all part of being a Christian."

"No matter what you do, we'll still love you." Bets let go of her handlebars and flung her arms out. "But better than that, Moon, so does Jesus."

"I don't see how." I looked up at the big Arizona sky. "Do you think he would want to hear from me now?"

Jessica slowed her bike down and stopped. "Jesus has been waiting the whole time, Moon."

I skidded to a stop, and Bets stopped beside me. "I'm ready, girlfriends. What do I say?"

"You just talk to Jesus like a friend, Moon. He hears everything. Ask him to forgive you. Ask Christ to be your Savior. He loves you, Moon. No matter how many times you goof up."

Taking a deep breath, I prayed out loud. I didn't care who heard me or what anyone thought of me anymore . . . not even Hubie Hoffmeister. A tear trickled down my cheek, and Bets and Jess hugged me. I felt weird. But I also felt great!

I hadn't gotten the pony I wanted so badly, but I realized I had found something worth more than all the ponies in Arizona. I had found friendship. I had found peace . . . and I had found Jesus Christ.

Acknowledgments:

I wish to thank the fine people who were so helpful in digging up the fine details that authenticate this book. Angela Williams of Maranatha Stables, Lou Bordelon of the Lazy B Stables, and Chris Jones of Live Oak Arabians—all true horsemen in their own right.

Also a special thank you to my editor, Alice Peppler. She saw the importance of this book first. I will always admire her understanding and expertise in fine tuning a novel for kids.

I would also like to extend a great big hug to the incredible kids at HCA elementary. They inspired me just when I needed a lift.